Planting ABC in a Garden of Memory

Rebecca and James McDonald

HOUSE OF LORE

Planting ABC
in a Garden of Memory

Requests for permission to make copies of any part of the work should be e-mailed to the following address:
Email: Business@HouseOfLore.net

ISBN: 978-0-9863151-5-2
First House of Lore paperback edition, 2015

www.SamiAndThomas.com

Dedicated to all those beginning the
adventure of reading.

Join Sami and Thomas as they take a walk through the ABC Garden of Memory!

A note to parents and teachers:
On the following page, place your finger on the garden gate and say the letter aloud. Then trace your way through the garden saying each letter as you come to it. Continue through the book paying special attention to the location of the letters, the rhyme, and all of the animals, objects, and insects on each page.

The more you visit the ABC Garden of Memory, the easier it will be to remember all of the letters.

Have fun planting your ABCs in a garden of memory!

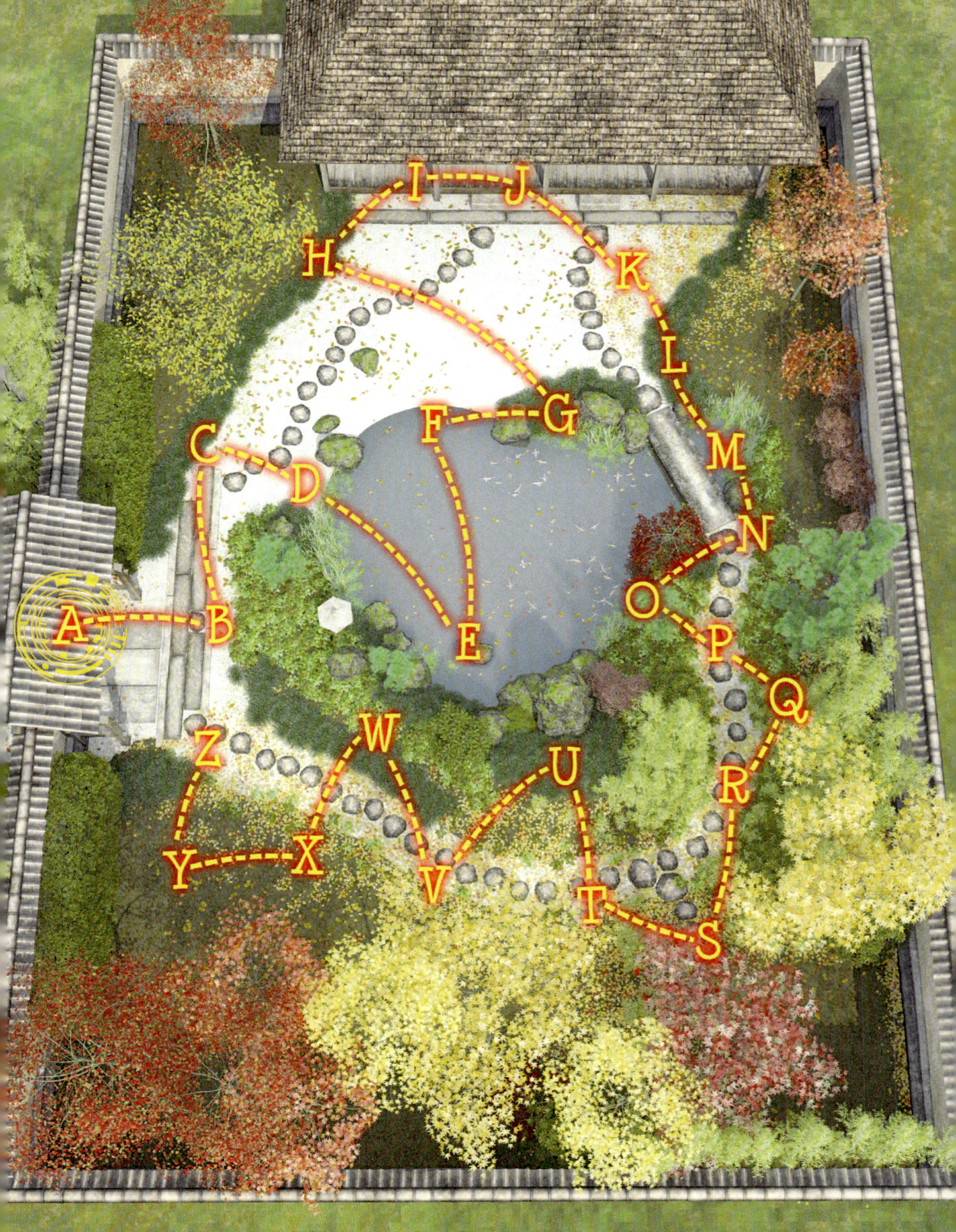

A is for an awesome apple, good for you and me.

B is for a bumble bee, as busy as can be.

C is for a clumsy cat, slipping on a stone.

D is for a dressed-up dog, dancing for his bone.

E is for an elegant elephant, balancing four eggs.

F is for a funny frog, stretching out his legs.

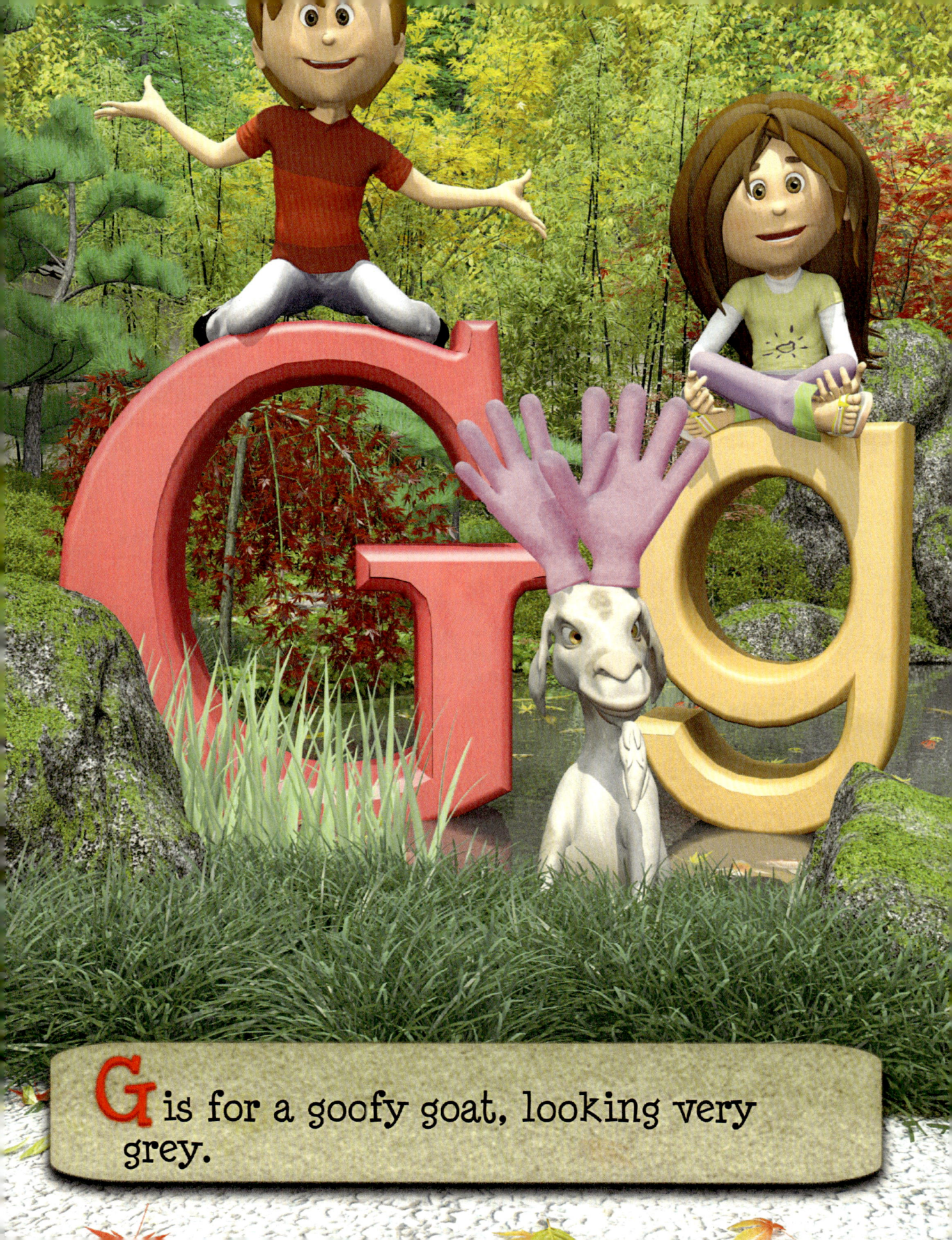

G is for a goofy goat, looking very grey.

H is for a happy horse, chewing on some hay.

I is for an icy ice cream, cool and sticky sweet.

J is for a jolly jester, jumping to her feet.

K is for a kooky kitten, watching her kite fly.

L is for a lofty ladder, reaching to the sky.

M is for a muddy mitt used to catch a ball.

N is for a nice new nest where baby birdies call.

O is for an offbeat ostrich, playing a crazy song.

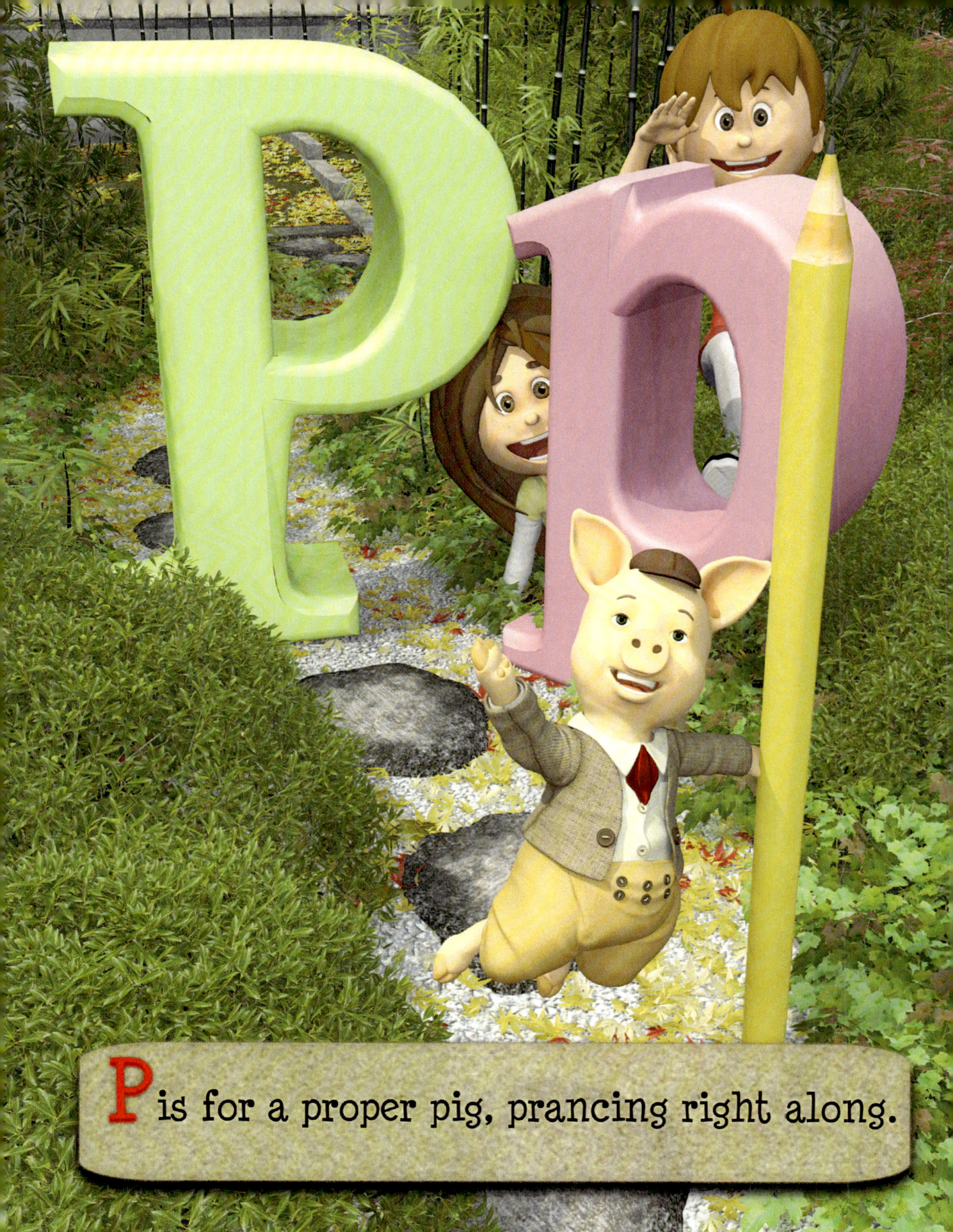

P is for a proper pig, prancing right along.

Q is for a quiet quilt, hanging on a line.

R is for a running rabbit, racing home to dine.

S is for a smelly skunk, standing all alone.

T is for a talking turtle with a telephone.

U is for a unique umbrella, floating in the air.

V is for a vexing vulture, losing all his hair.

W is for a wacky wolf, wobbling on a spoon.

X is for a xylophone, tapping out a tune.

Y is for a yellow yo-yo, spinning up and down.

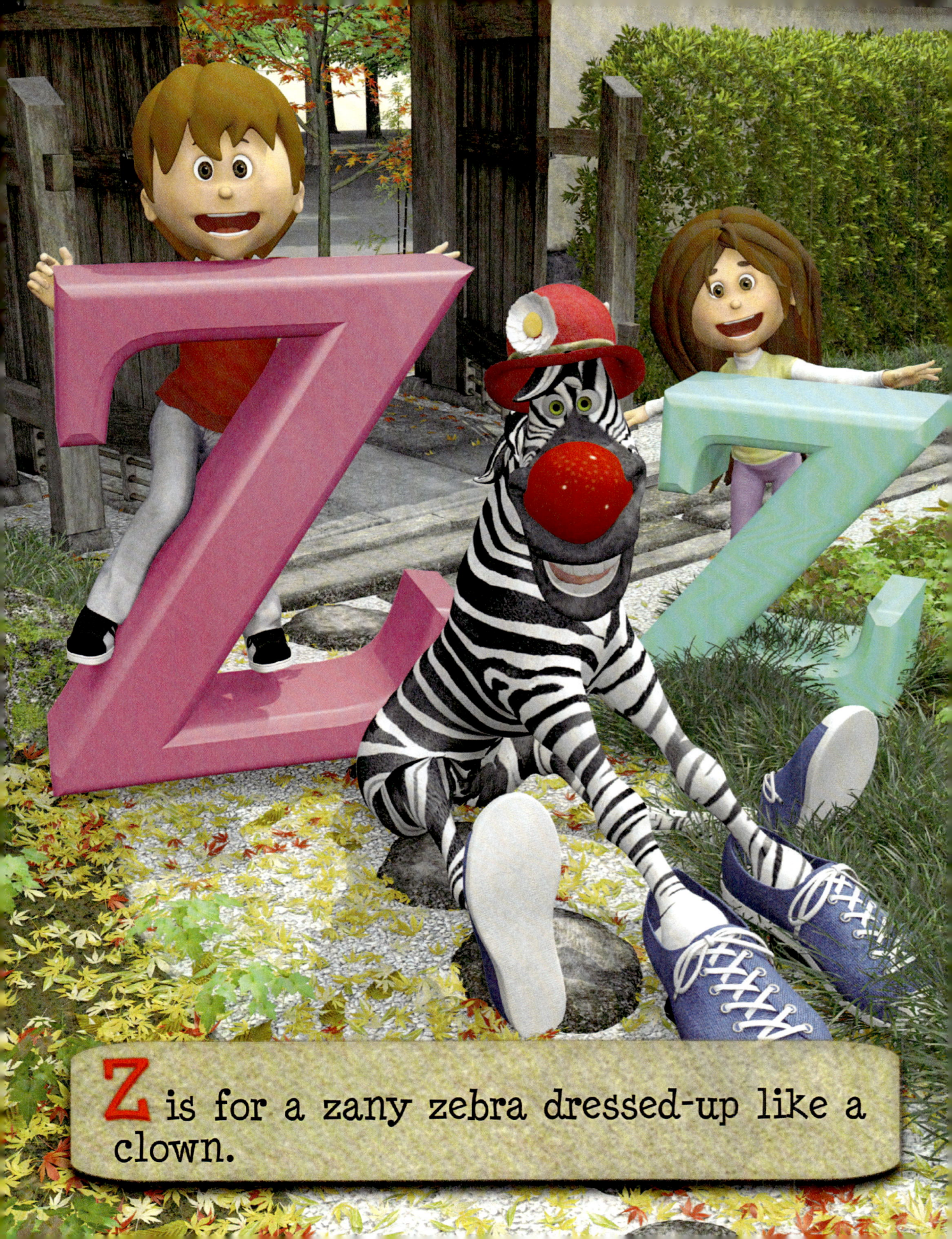

Z is for a zany zebra dressed-up like a clown.

Now let's see where the letters are on the map. Be sure to pay close attention.

M

M

N

N

O

O

P

P

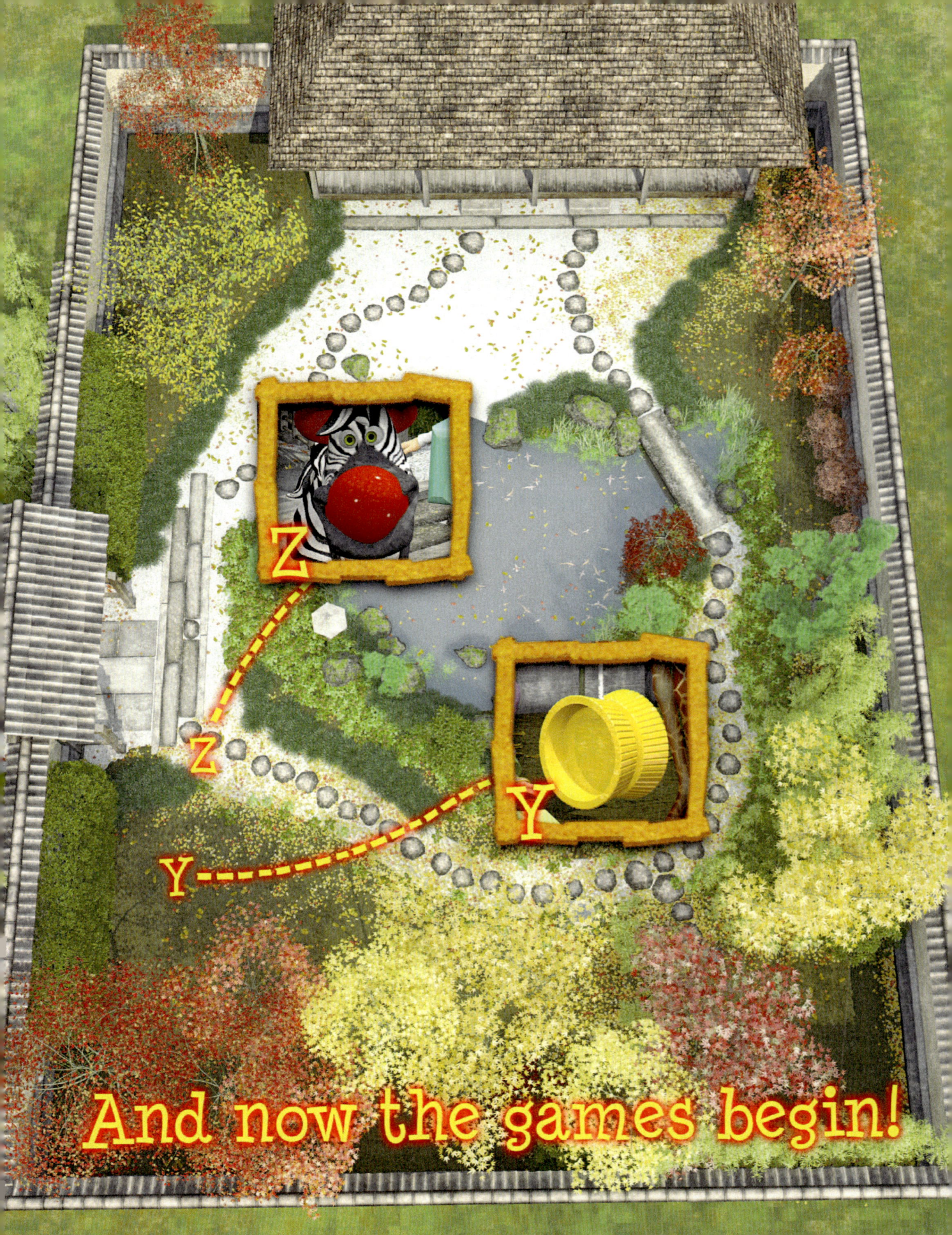

And now the games begin!

Play the games below to help your memory of the ABCs grow, until you become a Master of the ABC Garden of Memory.

Game 1: Where are the letters in the garden?

On the following page, place your finger on the garden gate and say what letter belongs in that spot. Then trace your way through the garden saying each letter as you come to its spot. When you remember where all the letters are then you have achieved the level of Builder of the ABC Garden of Memory. This may take some time, but with practice you will remember all of the letters.

Game 2: What animals, objects and insects go with each letter?

On the following page, place your finger on the garden gate and say what animals, objects, and insects started with the letter that belongs in that spot. Then trace your way through the garden and do the same for each of the other letters. When you remember all of the animals, objects, and insects for each letter then you have achieved the level of Keeper of the ABC Garden of Memory.

Game 3: Can you remember the rhyme?

On the following page, place your finger on the garden gate and repeat the rhyme for the letter that belongs in that spot. Then trace your way through the garden repeating the rhyme as you come to the next spot. When you remember the entire rhyme then you have achieved the level of Master of the ABC Garden of Memory.

Printable certificates of achievement
and the map of the
ABC Garden of Memory
can be found at
www.RainyDayPoems.com.

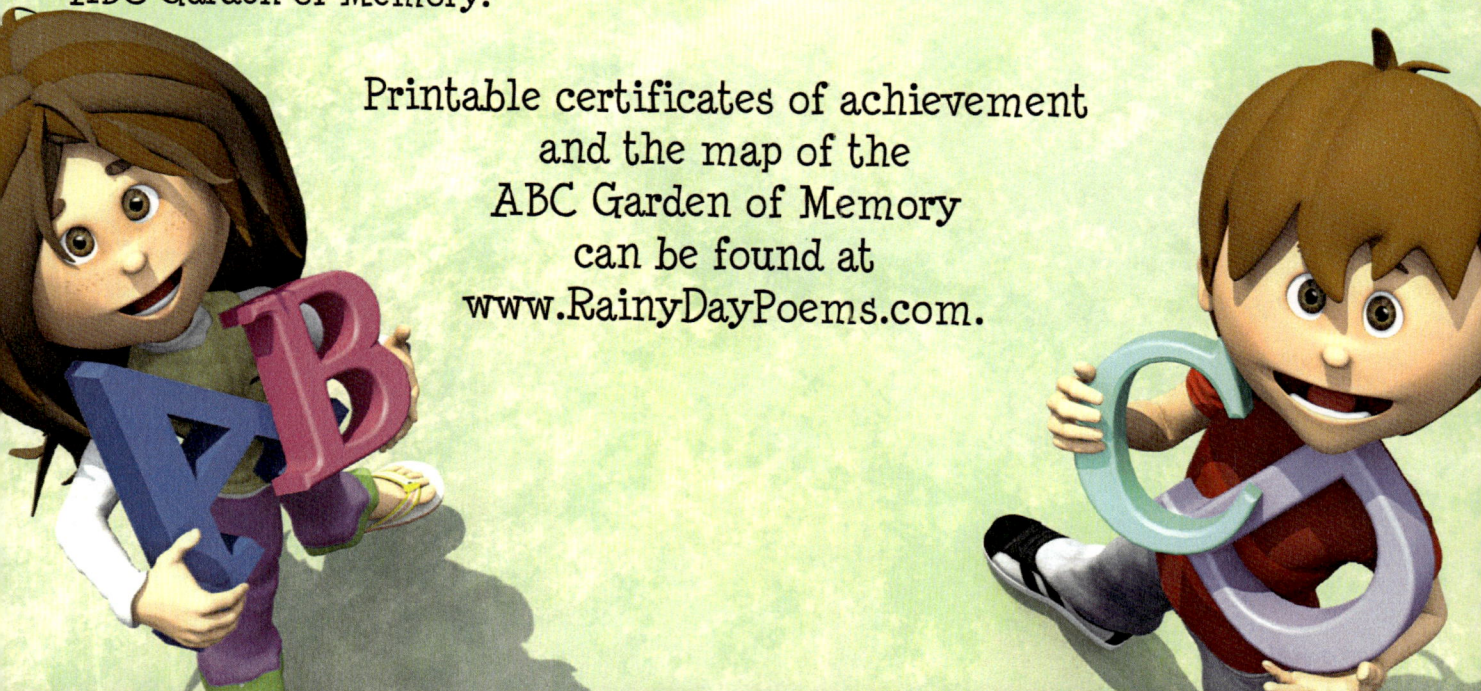

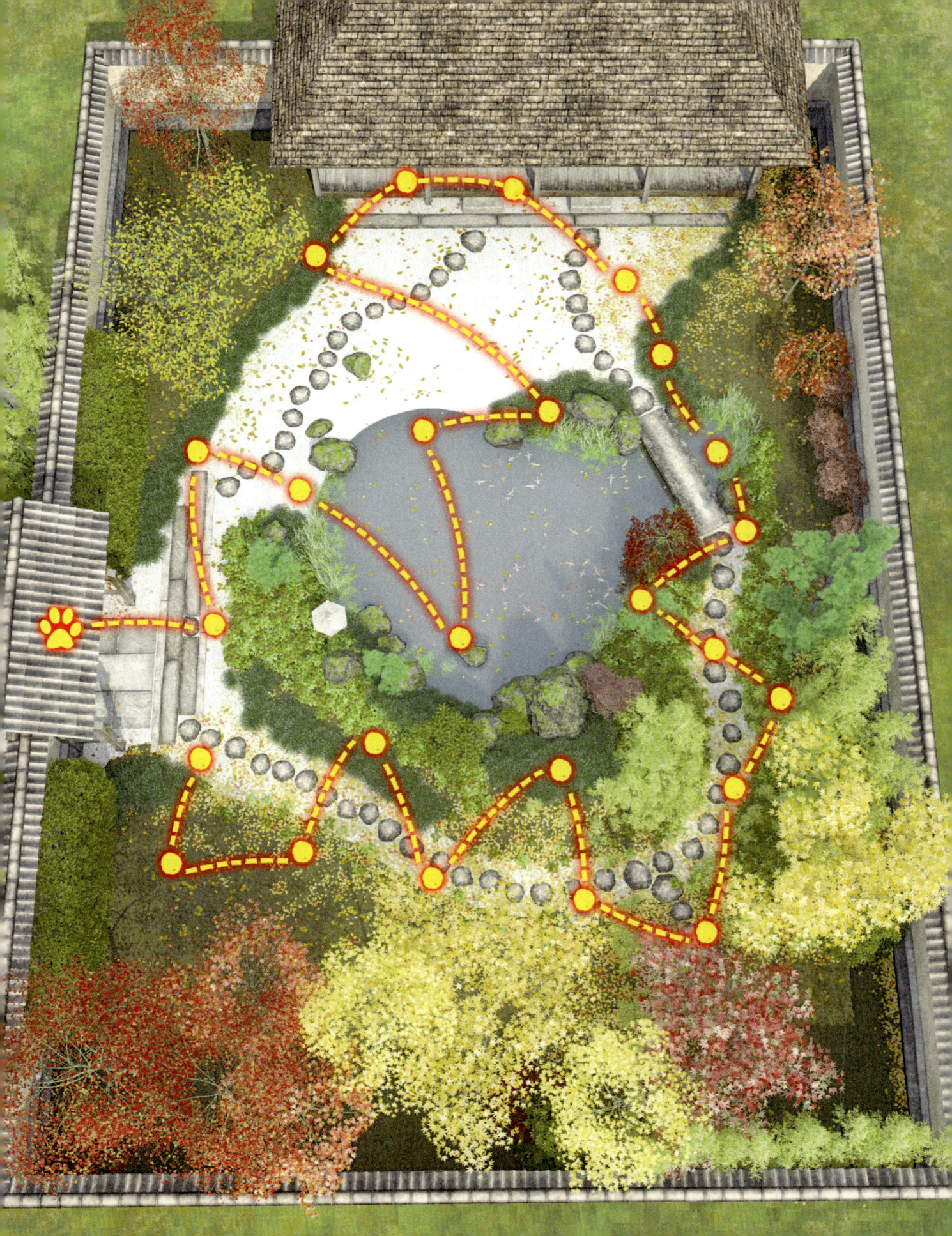

Welcome To The World Of Sami And Thomas

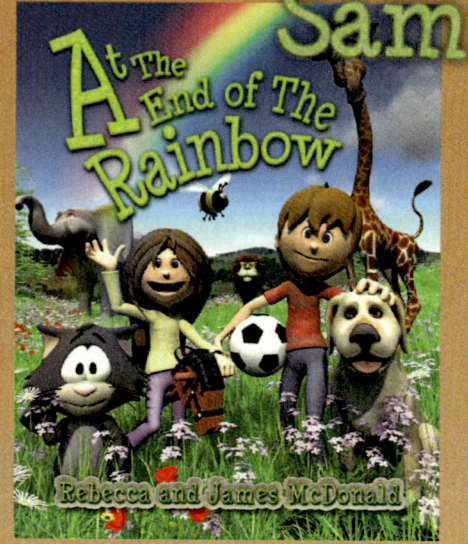

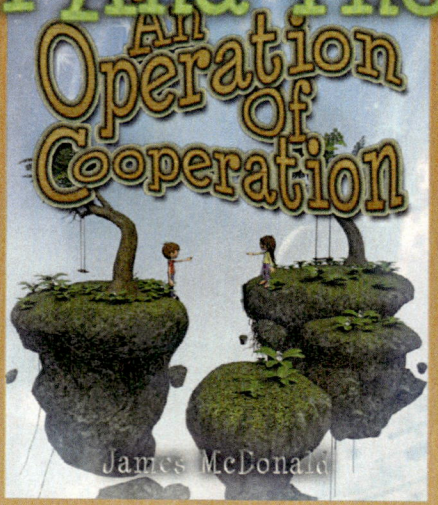

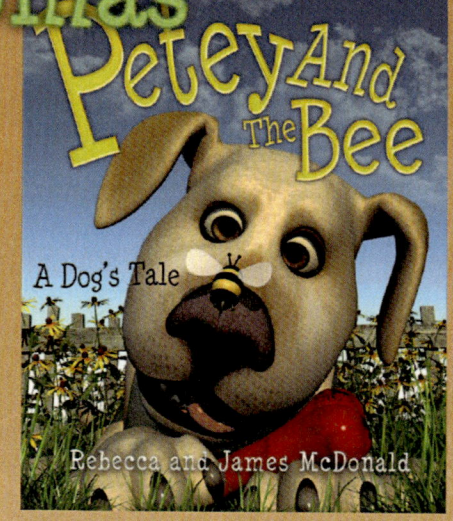

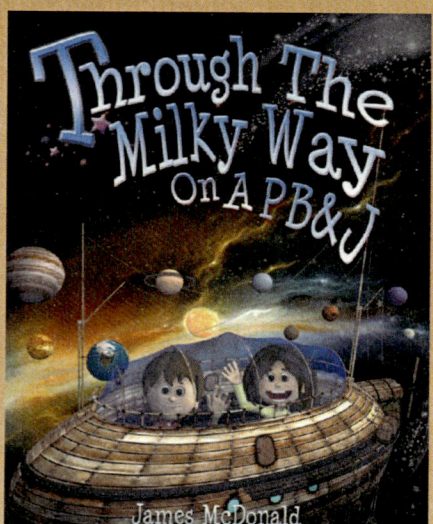

All books are available on Amazon.com

Check back often for the latest Sami and Thomas adventure, or non-fiction children's book.

Sami And Thomas
© HouseofLore

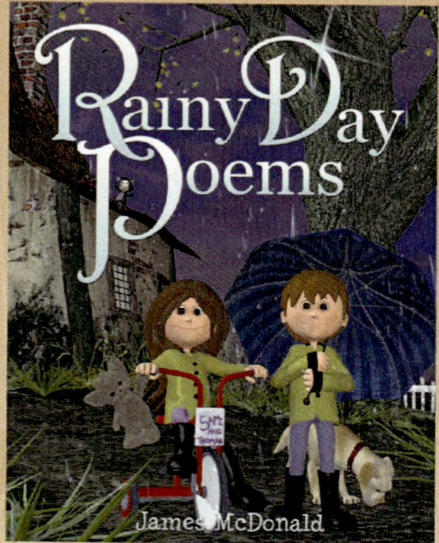